All Scripture is God-breathed and is useful for teaching, rebuking, correcting and training in righteousness.

—2 Timothy 3:16

ZONDERKIDZ

The Berenstain Bears® Let the Bible Be Your Guide

Copyright © 2011 by Berenstain Publishing, Inc.
Illustrations © 2011 by Berenstain Publishing, Inc.

Requests for information should be addressed to:
Zonderkidz, *Grand Rapids, Michigan 49530*

Library of Congress Cataloging-in-Publication Data

Berenstain, Jan, 1923–
    The Berenstain Bears : let the Bible be your guide / created by Stan and Jan ; with Mike
Berenstain.
        p. cm.
    ISBN 978-0-310-72714-9 (hardback)
    [1. Stories in rhyme. 2. Scouting (Youth activity)–Fiction. 3. White water canoeing–Fiction.
4. Bears–Fiction. 5. Christian life–Fiction.] I. Berenstain, Mike, 1951- II. Berenstain, Stan,
1923–2005. III. Title. IV Title: Let the Bible be your guide.
PZ8.3.B44925Bd 2011
[E] dc22   2010052434

Editor: Mary Hassinger
Art direction: Diane Mielke

Printed in China

11 12 13 14 15 16 /SCC/ 10 9 8 7 6 5 4 3 2 1

The Berenstain Bears®

Let the Bible Be Your Guide

by Stan and Jan Berenstain
with Mike Berenstain

ZONDERVAN.com/
AUTHORTRACKER
follow your favorite authors

ZONDERkidz

Beginning Reader

"Hooray!" said the Scouts.
"Hooray! Hooray!
We try for our
White Water badges today!"

"With life jackets, we are ready,
it's true.
And we're even bringing
our Bible too."

"One! Two! Three!"
said the Bear Scout crew
as they lifted up
their big canoe.

Scoutmaster Papa
had his own canoe.
The Scouts' was red.
Pa's was blue.

So off Papa went,
with his nephew, son, and daughter,
to test the Scouts' skills
on some white, white water.

"Papa, you don't have
a life jacket on!"
"A jacket for me?"
Papa said with a yawn.

"Since I swim like a fish,"
bragged Papa Bear,
"I'm as safe on Rapid River
as in my own lair!"

"Well, Uncle," said Fred,
very concerned,
"Proverbs says 'Let wise people listen
and add to what they've learned.'"

"At least take our troop's Bible,"
Brother Bear said.
"Please take it, Uncle,"
begged Cousin Fred.

"Thank you, thank you,
just the same,
but books and such
are not my game.

"I like my canoeing
wild and free!
Now into the river!
Follow me!"

"But those who listen to me
will live in safety,"
it says in the Holy Book.
"And Papa, take a look at our Good Deed Scout Guidebook:
'Rule Number One—
Do not canoe
where big currents run!'"

"Thank you for
that rule, my son.
But the bigger the current,
the bigger the fun!"

"Look out, Papa!
It's dangerous there!
That current is strong!
Please take care!"

"But I can swim like a fish.
So don't worry, daughter ..."

"Thanks, Scouts, for saving
both me and canoe!
What a great feeling!
What a grand view!"

"Papa, in the book of Proverbs we are told,
'Choose knowledge rather than gold.'
And the Scout Guidebook says:
'Rule Number Two—
Don't ever stand up
in a canoe!'"

"Please don't think me rude,
but for Rule Number Two
I have just three words:
Pooh! Pooh! And Poo—

"Hmm. What's that roaring sound I hear? There may be falls ahead, I fear."

"Relax, Bear Scouts.
Please calm your fears.
That roar is music
to my ears!"

"Look over there!
Papa Bear, look!
And listen to what else
it says in the book.

"The Scout Guidebook says:
'Rule Number Three—
Obey all signs
that you see!'"

"Rules and signs
mean nothing to me.
I like my canoeing
wild and free-e-e ...

"Thank you, Scouts,
I'm proud of you!
And truth to tell—

you've earned your White Water badges
and these Rescue ones, as well!
And just one more thing,
dear Scouts …
God's Guidebook is really swell!"

Whoever gives heed to instruction prospers,
and blessed is the one who trusts in the Lord.

—Proverbs 16:20